G.W Foote

Comic Bible Sketches
Volume 1

G.W Foote

Comic Bible Sketches
Volume 1

1st Edition | ISBN: 978-3-75237-655-5

Place of Publication: Frankfurt am Main, Germany

Year of Publication: 2020

Outlook Verlag GmbH, Germany.

Reproduction of the original.

COMIC BIBLE SKETCHES

By G. W. Foote

Part I.

INTRODUCTION.

English literature has its Comic Histories, its Comic Grammars, its Comic Geographies, and its Comic Law-Books, and Carlyle once prophesied that it would some day boast its Comic Bible. Tough as the fine old Sage of Chelsea was, he predicted this monstrosity with something of the horror a barbarian might feel at the thought of some irreverent fellow deliberately laughing at the tribal fetish. But what shocked our latter-day prophet so greatly in mere anticipation has partially come to pass. "La Bible Amusante" has had an extensive sale in France, and the infectious irreverence has extended itself to England. Notwithstanding that Mr. G. R. Sims, when he saw the first numbers of that abominable publication, piously turned up the whites of his eyes, and declared his opinion that no English Freethinker, however extreme, would think of reproducing or imitating them, there were found persons so utterly abandoned as not to scruple at this unparalleled profanity. Several of the French drawings were copied with more or less fidelity in the *Freethinker*, a scandalous print, as the Christians love to describe it, which has been prosecuted twice for Blasphemy, and whose editor, proprietor and publisher, have been punished respectively with twelve, nine and three months' imprisonment like common felons, all for the glory and honor of God, for the satisfaction of his dear Son, and for the vindication of the Holy Spirit. In many cases the French originals could not be reproduced in England, owing to their Gallic flavor. A Parisian artist, disporting himself among those highly moral histories in the Bible which our youths and maidens discover with unerring instinct, was not a spectacle which one could dare to exhibit before the pious and chaste British public; any more than an English poet could follow the lead of Evariste Parny in his "Guerre des Dieux" and "Les Amours de la Bible." But many others were free from this objection, and a selection of them served as a basis for the Freethinker artist to work on. A few were copied pretty closely;

some were elaborated and adapted to our national taste; while others furnished a central suggestion, which was treated in an independent manner. By-and-bye, as the insular diffidence wore off, and the minds of the Freethinker staff played freely on the subject, a new departure was taken; novel ideas were worked out, and Holy Writ was ransacked for fresh comicalities. Dullards prophesied a speedy exhaustion of Bible topics, but they did not know how inexhaustible it is in absurdities. Properly read, it is the most comical book in the world; and one might say of it, as Enobarbus says of Cleopatra, that Age cannot wither it, nor custom stale; it's infinite variety.

The following Comic Bible Sketches, which will be succeeded in due course by others, comprise all those worth preserving that appeared in the Freethinker before its editor, proprietor and publisher were imprisoned, including the drawings they were prosecuted for by that pious guinea: pig, Sir Henry Tyler, who had his dirty fingers severely rapped by Lord Coleridge, after spending several hundred pounds of somebody's money in an unsuccessful Blasphemy prosecution, in order to patch up his threadbare reputation, and perhaps also with a faint hope of cheating the Almighty into reserving him a front-seat ticket for the dress-circle in heaven.

The French Comic Bible prints under each illustration a few crisp lines of satiric narrative. This plan has its advantages; it allows, for instance, the writer's pen to curvet as well as the artist's pencil. But it is after all less effective than the plan we have adopted. We merely give each picture a comprehensive and striking title, and print beneath it the Bible text which is illustrated. By this means the satire is greatly heightened. Not even the sentences of a Voltaire could so illuminate and emphasise the grotesqueness of each topic as this juxtaposition of the solemnly absurd Scripture with the gaily absurd illustration.

The same spirit has animated us in designing the pictures. Our object has been to take the Bible text always as our basis, to include

3

no feature which is contradicted by it, and to introduce as many comicalities and anachronisms as possible consistently with this rule. We are therefore able to defy criticism. Bibliolators may vituperate us, persecute us, or imprison us, but they cannot refute us.. We can safely challenge them to prove that a single incident happened otherwise than we have depicted it. We can candidly say to them—"The thing must have happened in some way, as to which the Divine Word is silent; this is our view,—What is yours?" And we humbly submit that our speculations are as valid as our neighbors'. Nothing but the insanest bigotry in favor of their own conjectures could lead them to quarrel with us for expounding ours. If they can shame us with explicit disproofs from Holy Writ, let them do so; but what right have they to set up their carnal imaginings and uninspired theories as the ultimate criteria of truth?

Those who object to any employment of satire on "sacred" subjects should not go beyond the Preface of this book. It is not for them, nor are they for it; and they are warned in the hall of what they must expect in the various chambers. But if they neglect the warning they should take the responsibility. It will be simply indecent if they turn round afterwards and assail us with unmerited abuse.

For the sake of those who proceed in a spirit of impartial candor and honest inquiry, we beg to offer a little further explanation.

We honestly admit that our purpose is to discredit the Bible as the infallible word of God. Believing as we do, with Voltaire, that despotism can never be abolished without destroying the dogmas on which it rests, and that the Bible is the grand source and sanction of them all, we are profoundly anxious to expose its pretentions. The educated classes already see through them, and the upper classes credit them just as little, although they dare not openly profess a scepticism which would imperil their privileges. But the multitude are still left to the manipulation of priests, credulous victims of the Black Army everywhere arrayed against freedom and progress. It is to liberate these from thraldom that we labor, sacrifice and suffer. Without being indifferent to what the world calls success, we acknowledge the sovereignty of loftier aims. Compared with the advancement of Freethought everything else is to us of trivial moment. It may interest, and perhaps surprise, some to learn that for the famous Christmas Number of the Freethinker which was successfully prosecuted, the editor received absolutely nothing for his work except twelve months' imprisonment, while the then registered proprietor, who suffered nine months of the same fate, actually shared with him a pecuniary loss of five pounds. We are really in deadly earnest, like all the greater soldiers of freedom who preceded us; and we employ our smaller resources of satire, as such giants as Lucian, Rabelais, Erasmus, Voltaire and Heine used theirs, for ends that reach far forward into the mighty future, and affect the welfare of unimagined generations of mankind.

Now the masses do not read learned disquisitions; they have no leisure to make themselves adequately acquainted with the history of the Bible documents; nor can they study comparative religion, trace out the analogies between Christianity and older faiths, and realise how all the elaborate developments of doctrine and ritual in modern creeds have sprung from a few simple beliefs and practices of savage superstition. But they are conversant with one or two cardinal ideas of science, and they know the principles which underlie our daily life. What is called common sense (the logic of common experience) is their philosophy, and whoever seeks to move them must appeal to them through that. Strange as it may appear, it is that very common sense which the clergy dread far more than all the disclosures of learning and all the revelations of science; the reason being, that learning and science are the privilege of a few, while common sense is the possession of all, and affects the very foundations of spiritual and political tyranny.

Ridicule is a most potent form of common-sense logic. What is the *reductio ad absurdum* but an appeal to admitted truths against plausible falsehoods? Reducing a thing to an absurdity is simply showing its inconsistency with what is common to both sides in a dispute; and it frequently means the exposure of a gross contradiction to the principles of sanity. Laughter, too, as Hobbes pointed out, has always an element of pride or contempt; being invariably accompanied by a feeling of superiority to its object. Whoever laughs at an absurdity is above it. He looks down on it from a loftier altitude than argument can reach. The man who laughs is safe. He can never more be in danger, unless he suffers fatty degeneration of the heart or fattier degeneration of the head. Priestcraft nourishes hope in the scientific laboratory, and feels only faint misgivings in academic halls; but it pales and withers at the smile of scepticism, and hears in a low laugh the note of the trump of doom.

Ridicule can never injure truth. What it hurts must be false. Laugh at the multiplication-table as much as you please, and twice two will still make four.

Pictorial ridicule has the immense advantage of visualising absurdities. Lazy minds, or those accustomed to regard a subject with the reverence of prejudice, read without realising. But the picture supplies the deficiency of their imagination, translates words into things, and enables them to see what had else been only a vague sound.

Christians read the Bible without realising its wonders, allowing themselves to be cheated with words. Mr. Herbert Spencer has remarked that the image of the Almighty hand launching worlds into space is very fine until you try to form a mental picture of it, when it is found to be utterly irrealisable. In the same way, the Creation Story is passable until you image the Lord making a clay man and blowing up his nose; or the story of Samson until you picture him slaying file after file of well-armed soldiers with the jaw-bone of a costermonger's pony.

Let it be observed that these Comic Bible Sketches ridicule nothing but miracles. Mr. Mathew Arnold has said that the Bible miracles are only fairy tales (very poor ones, by the way) and their reign is doomed. We only seek to hasten their deposition. Whatever the Bible contains of truth, goodness and beauty, we prize as well as its blindest devotees. But this valuable deposit of antiquity would be more useful if cleared of the rubbish of superstition. It is not the good, but the evil parts of the Bible, that are supported by its supernaturalism. Why should civilised Englishmen go walking about in Hebrew Old-Clothes? Let us heed Carlyle's stern monition:—"The Jew old-clothes having now grown fairly pestilential, a poisonous incumbrance in the path of of men, burn them up with revolutionary fire."

A word in conclusion. The editor of the "Manchester Examiner," writing over the well-Known signature of "Verax," recently published a long article, censuring the policy of aggressive Freethought, and declaring that to laugh at the absurdities of the Bible was to insult the human race. We might as well, he said, laugh at our poor ancestors, the ancient Britons, for all their mistakes and follies. Well, when the ancient Jews are not only dead, but buried like the ancient Britons; when their mistakes and follies are no longer palmed off on unsuspecting children, and imposed on grown-up men and women, as divine immortal truths; we will cease ridiculing them, and devote our attention to worthier objects. What, would "Verax" say if an ancient Briton, dressed in a full suit of war-paint, were to walk through the Manchester streets, boasting himself the pink of fashion, and insulting peaceable citizens who refused to patronise his tailor? Would he not write a racy article on the absurd phenomenon, and ask why the police tolerated such a nuisance? In like manner we publish our Comic Bible Sketches, and summon the police of thought to remove those ancient Jews who still infest our mental thoroughfares.

April, 1885.

G. W. FOOTE

Enlarge to full size by clicking on any image.

ENLARGE

1.—DIVINE ILLUMINATION.
And God sa'd, Let there be light : and there was light.—GEN. i., 3.

ENLARGE

z.—THE LORD FIXING UP THE SUN AND MOON.
And God made two great lights . . . And God set them in the
firmament of the heaven.—GEN. i., 16, 17.

ENLARGE

5.—MAKING MAN.

And God said, Let us make man in our image, after our likeness.—GEN. i., 26.

ENLARGE

4.—THE LORD OF CREATION.
And God said . . . have dominion . . . over every living thing that
moveth upon the earth.—GEN. i., 28.

ENLARGE

5.—JEHOVAH'S DAY OF REST.

For in six days the Lord made heaven and earth, and on the seventh day he rested, and was refreshed.—Exodus xxxi., 17.

ENLARGE

6.—ORIGINAL SIN.

Hast thou eaten of the tree whereof I commanded thee that thou shouldst not eat ?—GEN. iii., 11.

ENLARGE

7.—THE FIRST TAILOR.
Unto Adam also and to his wife did the Lord God make coats of
skins, and clothed them.—GEN. iii., 21.

ENLARGE

8.—THE KICK OUT OF PARADISE.

Therefore the Lord God sent him forth from the garden of Eden, to till the ground from whence he was taken.—GEN. iii. 23.

ENLARGE

9.—A CARNIVOROUS GOD

Cain brought of the fruit of the ground an offering unto the Lord.
And Abel, he also brought of the firstlings of his flock and of the fat
thereof. And the Lord had respect unto Abel and to his offering;
But unto Cain and to his offering he had not respect.—GEN. iv., 3—5.

ENLARGE

10.—THE FIRST RELIGIOUS MURDER.

And the Lord said unto Cain, Where is Abel thy brother ? And he said, I know not : Am I my brother's keeper ?—GEN. iv., 9.

ENLARGE

11.—ENOCH MOUNTING.

And Enoch walked with God : and he was not ; for God took him.—
GEN. v., 24.

ENLARGE

18

12.—FATHER METHUSELAH.

And Methuselah lived an hundred eighty and seven years, and
begat Lamech.—GEN. v., 25.

ENLARGE

13.—RELIGIOUS COURTSHIP.

The sons of God saw the daughters of men that they were fair.—
Gen. vi., 2.

ENLARGE

I4.—NOAH'S ARK.

And Noah went in, and his sons, and his wife, and his sons' wives with him, into the ark . . . The same day were all the fountains of the great deep broken up, and the windows of heaven were opened.— GEN. vii., 7, 11.

ENLARGE

15.—EMPTYING THE MENAGERIE

And the ark . . . rested upon the mountains of Ararat. . . . And Noah
went forth, and his sons, and his wife, and his sons' wives with him
Every beast, every creeping thing, and every fowl.—Gen. viii., 4, 18, 19

ENLARGE

22

16.—THE ORIGINAL TELEPHONE.

And God spake unto Noah.—GENESIS ix., 8.

ENLARGE

17.—FIXING THE RAINBOW.
I do set my bow in the clouds.—Gen. ix., 13.

ENLARGE

18.—ABRAHAM'S ORDEAL.

And it came to pass after these things, that God did tempt
Abraham. . . . And he said, Take now thy son, thine only son Isaac,
whom thou lovest, and get thee into the land of Moriah; and offer
him there for a burnt offering.—Gen. xxii., 1, 2.

ENLARGE

19.—A MISS AND A HIT.

And the angel of the Lord called unto him out of heaven, and said,
Abraham, Abraham; and he said, Here am I. . . . And he said, Lay
not thine hand upon the lad, neither do thou anything unto him.—
Gen. xxii., 11, 12.

ENLARGE

20.—JACOB CHEATING HIS FATHER.

And Jacob went near unto Isaac his father; and he felt him, and said, Thy voice is Jacob's voice, but the hands are the hands of Esau. —Gen. xxvii., 19—22.

ENLARGE

21.—JACOB'S LADDER.

And he dreamed, and behold a ladder set up on the earth, and the top of it reached to heaven: and behold the angels of God ascending and descending on it. And, behold, the Lord stood above it.—Gen. xxviii., 12, 18.

ENLARGE

22.—THE LORD'S WRESTLING MATCH.

And when he saw that he prevailed not against him, he touched the
hollow of his thigh ; and the hollow of Jacob's thigh was out of joint
as he wrestled with him.—GENESIS XXXII., 25.

ENLARGE

23.—WRESTLING WITH AN ANGEL.

And when he saw that he prevailed not against him, he touched the hollow of his thigh ; and the hollow of Jacob's thigh was out of joint as he wrestled with him.—Genesis xxxii, 25.

ENLARGE

24.—ÁTTEMPTED ASSASSINATION of MOSES by JEHOVAH.

And it came to pass by the way in the inn, that the Lord met him,
nd sought to kill him.—Exodus iv., 24.

ENLARGE

25.—BOILS IN EGYPT.

And the magicians could not stand before Moses because of the boils; for the boil was upon the magicians, and upon all the Egyptians Ex. ix.. 11.

ENLARGE

26.—A MEAT (?) OFFERING.

And ne put the altar of burnt offering by the door of the tabernacle of the tent of the congregation, and offered upon it the burnt offering and the meat offering; a: the Lord commanded Moses.—Ex xl., 29.

ENLARGE

33

27 — BALAAM'S ASS.

And the ass saw the angel of the Lord standing in the way, and his sword drawn in his hand. . . . And the Lord opened the mouth of the ass, and she said unto Balaam, What have I done unto thee, that thou hast smitten me these three times?—Numbers xxii. 23, 28.

ENLARGE

28.—JEHOVAH THROWING STONES.

The Lord cast down great stones from heaven upon them unto Azekah and they died.—JOSH. x., 11

ENLARGE

29.—JOSHUA STOPPING THE SUN.

So the sun stood still in the midst of heaven, and hasted not to go down about a whole day.—Josh. x., 13.

ENLARGE

[30.—UNDER THE JEW JUDGES.
Monday morning in Jerusalem three thousand years ago. A Hittite
before the Court.

ENLARGE

31.—A BIBLE HERO.

And after him was Shamgar the son of Anath, which slew of the Philistines six hundred men with an ox goad: and he also delivered Israel.—JUDGES iii., 31.

ENLARGE

32.—SAMSON AND THE FOXES.

And Samson went and caught three hundred foxes, and took fire-brands, and turned tail to tail, and put a firebrand in the midst between two tails. And when he had set the brands on fire, he let them go into the standing corn of the Philistines.—Judges xv., 4, 5.

ENLARGE

33.—A FEAT OF STRENGTH.

And Samson . . . arose at midnight and took the doors of the gate of
the city and the two posts, and went away with them bar and all, and put
them upon his shoulders and carried them up to the top of an hill.—
JUDGES xvi., 3.

ENLARGE

34.—THE CONSECRATION OF SAUL.

Then Samuel took a vial of oil and poured it upon his head.—
1 Sam x. 1.

ENLARGE

35.—THE CHAMPION GIANT-SLAYER.

So David prevailed over the Philistine with a sling and with a stone
and smote the Philistine, and slew him.—1 Sam. xvii., 50.

ENLARGE

86.—DAVID DANCING BEFORE THE LORD.

Michal Saul's daughter looked through a window, and saw King David leaping and dancing before the Lord; and she despised him . . . who uncovered himself to day in the eyes of the handmaids of his servants.—2 SAM. vi., 16, 20.

ENLARGE

37.—ELIJAH'S LITTLE FEAST.

And the word of the Lord came unto him, saying, Get thee hence,
and turn thee eastward, and hide thyself by the brook Cherith, that is
before Jordan. . . . And the ravens brought him bread and flesh
1 KINGS xvii., 2, 3, 6.

ENLARGE

36.—ELISHA AND THE BEARS.

As he was going by the way, there came forth little children out of the city, and mocked him, and said unto him, Go up, thou bald head . . . And he . . . cursed them in the name of the Lord. And there came forth two she bears . . . and tare forty and two children of them.—2 KINGS ii., 23, 24

ENLARGE

39.—IN THE FIERY FURNACE.

I see four men loose, walking in the midst of the fire, and they have no hurt; and the form of the fourth is like the Son of God.—DAN. iii., 25.

Lightning Source UK Ltd.
Milton Keynes UK
UKHW012210100820
367994UK00009B/1240